VOLCANO

river of lava

NATIONAL GEOGRAPHIC NATURE LIBRARY

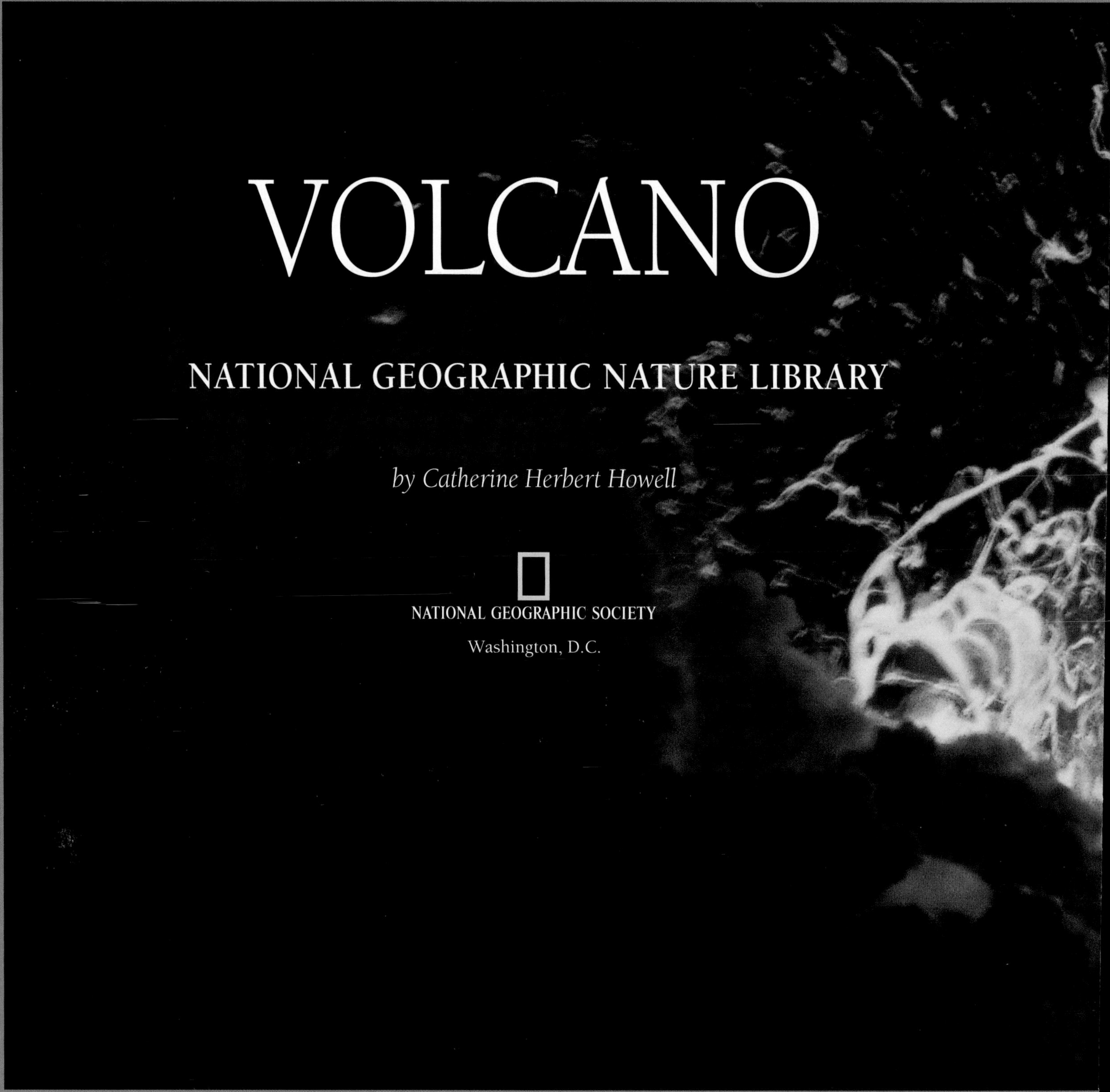

VOLCANO

NATIONAL GEOGRAPHIC NATURE LIBRARY

by Catherine Herbert Howell

NATIONAL GEOGRAPHIC SOCIETY

Washington, D.C.

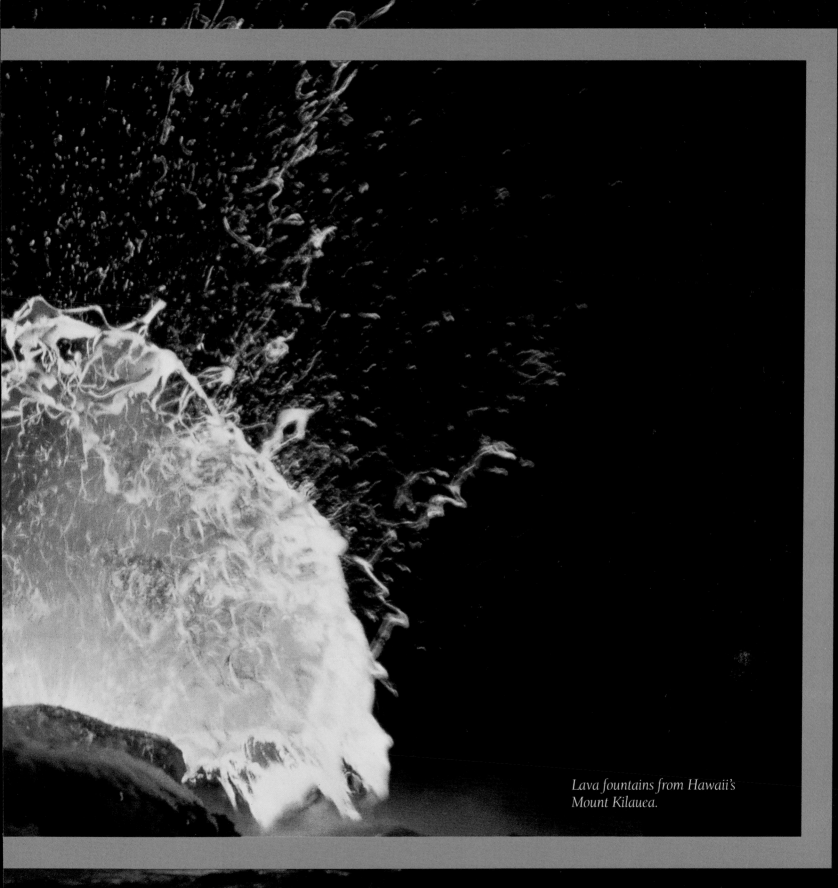

Lava fountains from Hawaii's Mount Kilauea.

Table of Contents

aa lava

tube worms

Long Valley Caldera, California

Shishaldin Volcano, Alaska

ashfall from Mount Pinatubo, Philippines

fireweed

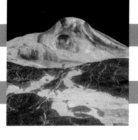
Devils Postpile, California

Mount Kilimanjaro, Africa

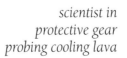
Maat Mons, Venus

scientist in protective gear probing cooling lava

WHAT IS A VOLCANO?

If the word "volcano" makes you think of a mountain with fire gushing from its summit, you've got the concept. Volcanic activity starts with molten rock, called magma, that forms deep inside the Earth. Magma (MAG-muh) collects in a layer of rock called the mantle. Heat and pressure deep within the Earth cause magma, together with hot gases, to burst through the planet's crust, or outer layer, creating the fiery mountains that are volcanoes as well as other landforms.

In this book you will learn about the powerful force of volcanoes and what they can teach us about how the Earth is made. Here are some facts to get you started:

- VOLCANIC ACTIVITY, or VOLCANISM, has shaped much of the Earth's surface, including the bottom of the oceans.
- Volcanoes helped create Earth's ATMOSPHERE.
- MAGMA that breaks through Earth's crust is called LAVA.
- Volcanoes occur on EVERY CONTINENT, including Antarctica.
- Volcanoes often occur together with EARTHQUAKES.

mid-ocean ridge

rift

ocean

Antarctic volcano

new crust

crust

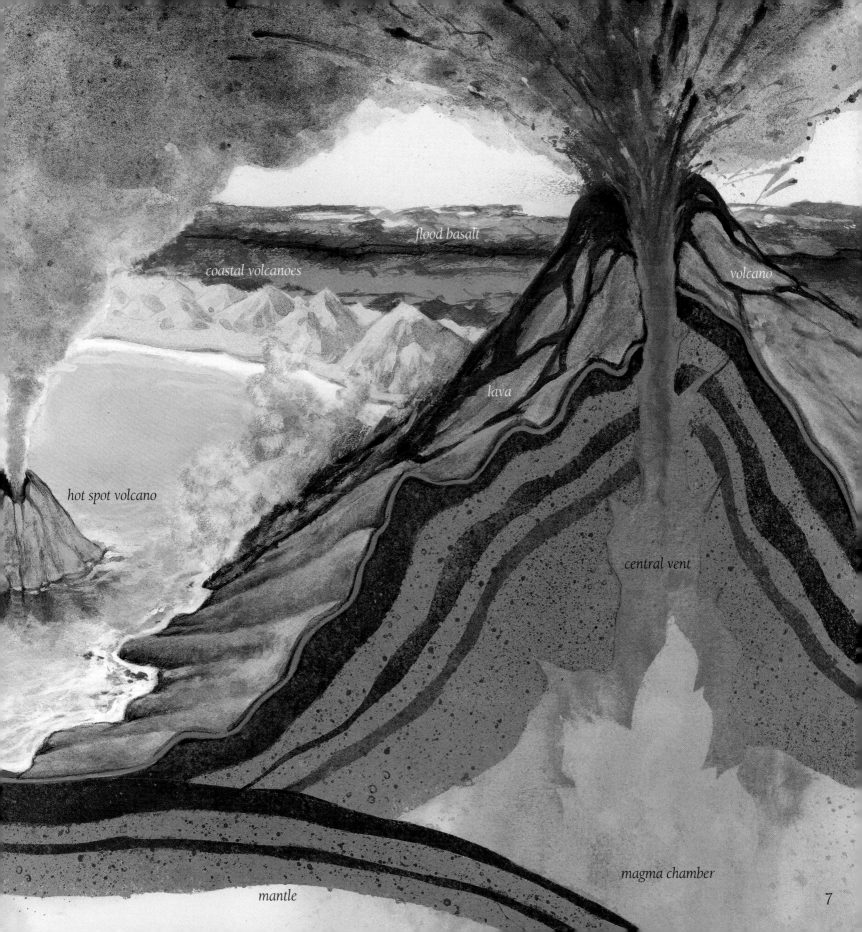

flood basalt

coastal volcanoes

volcano

lava

hot spot volcano

central vent

magma chamber

mantle

7

Creeping Crust

While the whole Earth spins on its axis, the ground beneath you is also moving. The outer shell of Earth, called the crust, is broken into immense slabs of rock called plates. All the land—including the ocean floor— sits on those plates. For millions of years the plates have been moving around very slowly. They touch, sometimes slide under one other, or pull apart. Where plates interact, big changes in the land above usually occur, and volcanic activity is often part of the picture.

WAVE GOODBYE
In 1964 the Alaska port of Valdez was destroyed by a tsunami (tsu-NAH-me), a giant sea wave. Volcanic eruptions and earthquakes that make the ocean floor buckle often cause tsunamis.

NORTH AMERICAN
PLATE
EURASIAN PLATE
Ring of Fire
JUAN DE FUCA PLATE
GORDA PLATE
ARABIAN PLATE
AFRICAN
PLATE
INDIAN
PLATE
PHILIPPINE PLATE
CAROLINE PLATE
PACIFIC
PLATE
RIVERA PLATE
CARIBBEAN PLATE
AFRICAN PLATE
COCOS PLATE
SOMALI PLATE
GALÁPAGOS MICROPLATE
SOUTH
AMERICAN
PLATE
AUSTRALIAN PLATE
EASTER MICROPLATE
NAZCA PLATE
Ring of Fire
JUAN FERNÁNDEZ MICROPLATE
Ring of Fire
SOUTH AMERICAN PLATE
SCOTIA PLATE
ANTARCTIC PLATE

- Volcano
○ Hot spot
⌒ Plate boundary

RETURN TO SENDER ▶
Red-hot lava meets the sea on the Big Island of Hawaii. A hot spot in the middle of the Pacific plate created the Hawaiian volcano Kilauea.

A WHOLE NEW WORLD
Volcanoes often occur at the edges of plates. The most active volcanic area in the world is called the Ring of Fire. It lies on the rim of the Pacific plate, the rock slab carrying the Pacific Ocean floor. As the Pacific plate dives under the edge of a continental plate, rock melts, fueling volcanoes on land. Hot spots, areas where magma burns through the middle of a plate, exist far from plate boundaries and create volcanoes on land and under the sea.

Earth Erupts!

Earth's magma factory lies mainly in the mantle, a layer of very hot rock sandwiched between the planet's outer crust and the inner core. High temperatures there melt some of the rock, creating magma. It also forms in the lower part of Earth's crust. Magma collects in large underground reservoirs called chambers, where heat, pressure, and gases may cause it to erupt to the surface.

The temperature of magma can reach 2200°F.

TURN UP THE HEAT
Magma builds up in a large chamber beneath a volcano. It erupts through channels within the volcano.

PREHISTORIC SHOWERS
Four billion years ago, volcanoes began erupting on Earth. Over time, water vapor and other gases they discharged from the interior of the planet created Earth's atmosphere and its earliest oceans.

FIRE DOWN SOUTH
No part of Earth's crust is too cold for volcanic fire. Smoke rises from Mount Erebus on the continent of Antarctica.

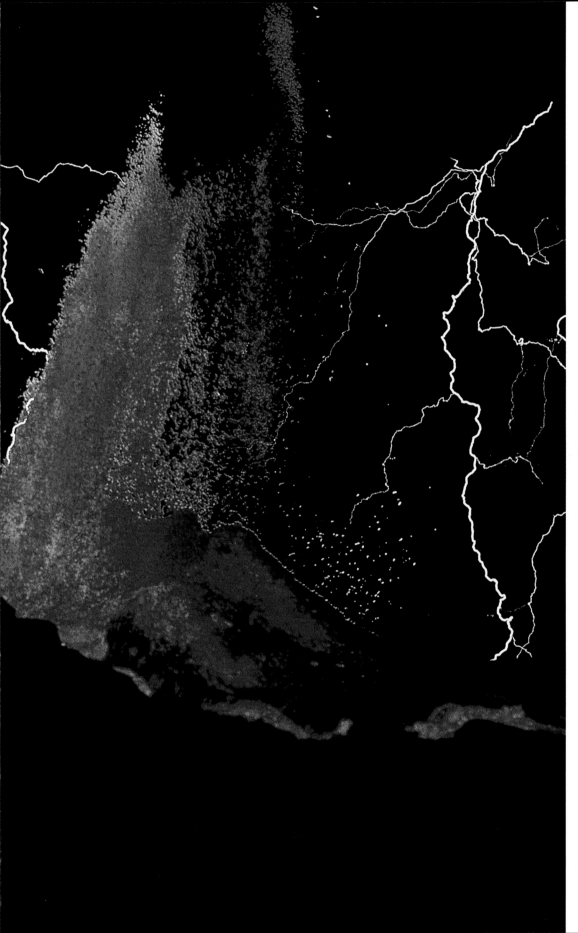

LIGHT MY FIRE
Tiny particles of ash from an eruption create electricity as they rub against the surrounding air. When enough electricity accumulates, a bolt of lightning leaps through the air.

HOT STUFF
Lava isn't the only product of a volcanic eruption. Ash, gases, and rock from the surrounding area are part of the fiery mix.

11

Cone Heads

All volcanic mountains are not created equal. The shape of a volcano depends on many things, including the type of magma that fuels it and the internal plumbing of the volcano. Some volcanoes start with a central column that sends magma up and out, forming a crater at the summit. Eventually, sideways pipes may develop from the center and channel the magma out through cracks in the volcano's sides.

MIGHTY FLOOD
Millions of years ago immense flows of runny lava gushed from cracks in the Earth in eruptions known as flood basalts, named for the kind of rock the lava made as it cooled.

LAYER CONE ▼
Japan's Mount Fuji is a composite cone, a volcano that grew from alternating layers of lava and ash.

FANT-ASH-TIC ▲
Cinder cone volcanoes, like Mexico's Paricutín, usually rise rapidly. Cinders, or small fragments of rock, build up quickly, so cinder cones usually have steep sides.

◄ SHIELD ME
Thin, runny lava builds shield volcanoes, typical of Hawaii. The lava travels far before it hardens and cools into shallow slopes.

12

Active volcanoes still erupt. Volcanoes that haven't blown up in a while are asleep, or dormant. Extinct volcanoes are finished erupting.

TAKE IT EASY

Lava flows almost straight down from Mauna Loa, a shield volcano on Hawaii. Hawaiians think Mauna Loa is the home of Pele, goddess of volcanoes.

Volcanoes Rock

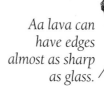

Aa lava can have edges almost as sharp as glass.

What's in a name? If the name is "lava," a lot of different things. Lava is made of minerals and dissolved gases. These help determine what the lava will look like as it hardens and becomes rock. One of the minerals in lava is silica, the same one that forms most sand. Lava with a lot of silica is thick and flows slowly. Lava with less silica tends to be thinner and flows quickly.

NAME THAT ROCK

Mineral composition, amount of gases, and rate of cooling contribute to the different looks of rocks created by lava.

OUCH-OUCH

Slow-flowing lava creates aa (AH-AH), hardened lava with a jagged surface. So many volcanoes dot the Hawaiian islands that people have named the different types of lava. "Aa" comes from sounds people make when they walk on this type of lava.

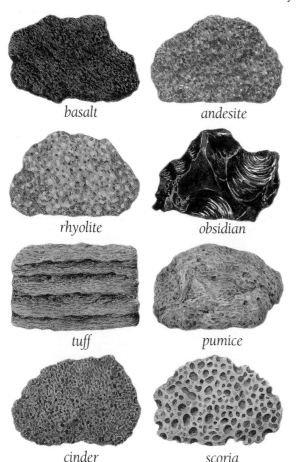

basalt

andesite

rhyolite

obsidian

tuff

pumice

cinder

scoria

SWEET DREAMS

When fast-flowing hot pahoehoe (pa-HOY-hoy) meets the ocean, it cools quickly, forming segments of rock called pillow lava because of their shape.

ROUND 'EM UP ▶

Thin and fast-flowing, pahoehoe lava takes on a smooth ropy shape. As it cools and hardens, pahoehoe forms a skin that folds into coils.

Alternative Rock

Lava is only one product of a volcanic eruption. As a volcanic mountain erupts, parts of the mountain itself get blown to bits. Geologists sort these pieces of rock, called ejecta, by size. The smallest pieces are called ash. Rocks less than two and a half inches across are called lapilli (luh-PIH-lee), which means "little stones" in Latin. Larger chunks of ejecta are called blocks.

BOMBS AWAY
When erupting volcanoes send out blobs of molten lava with great force, they may cool quickly into lava "bombs." Some lava bombs are larger than a school bus.

Some bombs travel several miles before hitting the ground.

TOOTHY TUFA
Tufa (TYEW-fuh) towers in California's Mono Lake grow from mineral deposits in hot springs. Magma heats the water containing minerals, which bubbles back up to the surface as hot springs.

DARK SHORES

Wind and water wear away black volcanic rock on the coast of Hawaii. Lava that cooled very quickly created many dark-sand beaches on the volcanic islands.

COLOR MY WORLD

Different colors reflect the different kinds of minerals deposited by steam at a volcanic vent: iron red, sulfur yellow, and calcium white.

ROCK TO ROCK

Rock of the Earth's crust created by undersea volcanism slides under the edge of a continent. The rock melts, making new magma that erupts again.

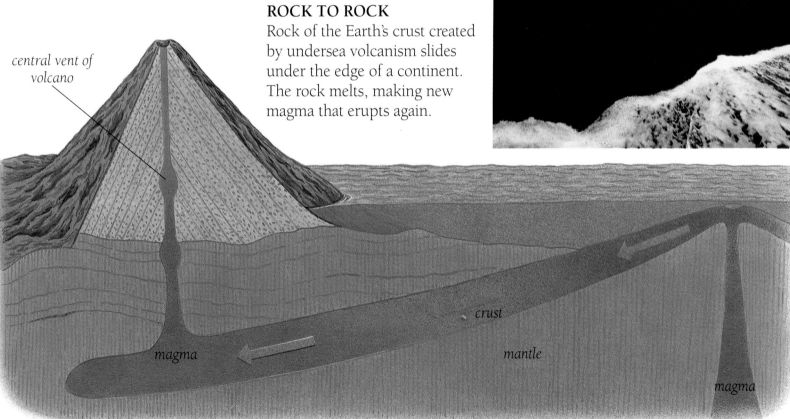

central vent of volcano

magma

crust

mantle

magma

Blasts from the Past

For millions of years volcanoes have shaped the surface of the Earth. Volcano-generated mountains, layers of lava, and thick deposits of ash cover many parts of the world, even where there are no active volcanoes today. Ancient floods of lava poured over hundreds of miles to create the Columbia River Plateau, North America's largest volcanic landform. Super-hot ash, in some places up to a thousand feet thick, once covered a large part of the western United States.

A RIVER RUNS THROUGH IT
The Snake River flows through deposits of volcanic ash in Idaho, the result of eruptions some 13 million years ago. Immense magma chambers blew existing mountains into ash that blanketed most of the southern part of the state. Some scientists think the crash of an enormous meteorite triggered the eruptions that ripped through the area.

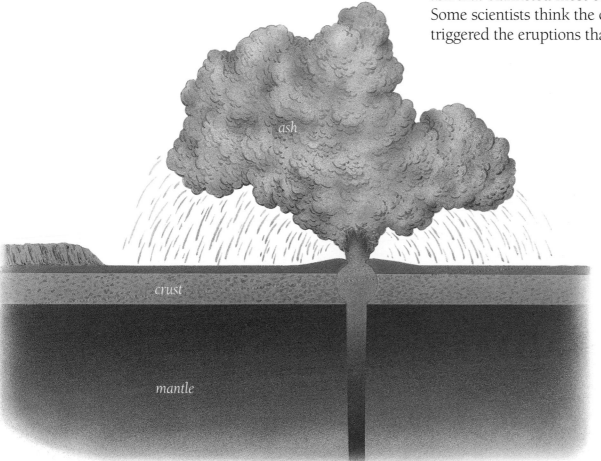

ash

crust

mantle

SECOND ACT
Lava flowed for two million years to make the Columbia River Plateau. Then, about 600,000 years ago, violent eruptions of volcanic ash left a thick deposit over thousands of square miles. Volcanism not only builds mountains and plateaus, but also shapes the planet in subtle ways. Today, layers of ash deposits along the Columbia River Plateau are visible where builders have scraped away the land to construct roads.

The cones and bowl-shaped depressions at Craters of the Moon National Monument in Idaho look so much like the surface of the moon that astronauts trained there. Massive lava flows created this lunar look-alike.

LAVA LAND
Lava that flowed from ancient cracks in the ground meets fertile wheat fields in Idaho. The minerals in volcanic rock make rich soil.

2 Under the Sea

If you think by now that land is an erupting kind of place, consider the bottom of the ocean. Most of the volcanic features that occur on land can be found under the sea—often in bigger and more spectacular form. At rifts, immense cracks in the ocean floor where plates are moving apart, lava wells up through the cracks between them, creating new seafloor. Lava has also built a chain of mostly undersea mountains that circles the Earth. Called the Mid-Ocean Ridge, the huge chain stretches more than 40,000 miles.

black smoker

tube worms

giant clams

20

LIFE ON THE BOTTOM
The research vessel *Alvin* hovers near black smokers, natural chimneys made of minerals deposited when water heated inside the Earth shoots out of openings in the ocean floor. The minerals nourish creatures around the smokers. Behind *Alvin*, lava has formed mountains of the Mid-Ocean Ridge, largest landform on Earth. The mountains average 10,000 feet in height.

mid-ocean ridge

Alvin

rift

21

Life-giving Vents

Volcanic forces beneath the sea make it possible for creatures to live without benefit of the sun's light. These life-forms survive near vents, openings in the seafloor along the rifts where plates are separating. Super-hot water filled with minerals and heated by magma within the Earth spurts from the vents. The minerals provide food for tiny organisms called bacteria. The bacteria, in turn, nourish giant tube worms, large clams, and spider crabs that cluster around the vents. Scientists did not discover these new life-forms in the dark and cold depths of the oceans until the 1970s.

Some 250 different types of microscopic bacteria provide food for the creatures that survive near undersea vents.

Tube worms lack mouths and stomachs. Bacteria living inside the worms make food for them from vent chemicals.

Foot-long clams filter food from the billion bacteria that live in each quart of vent water.

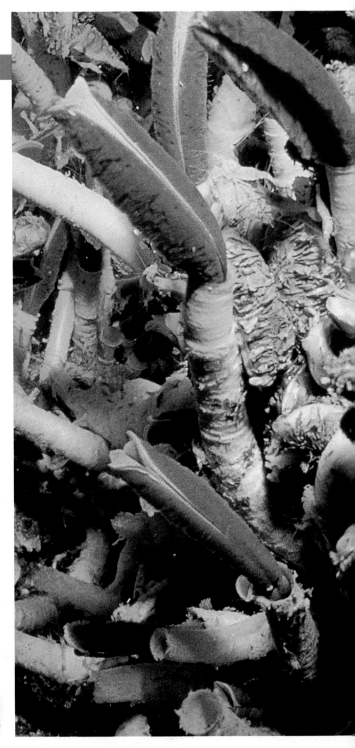

TUBULAR
Resembling long, wriggling lipsticks, giant tube worms wave in the current of their deep-sea home. These creatures thrive at the volcanic vents, growing up to 12 feet in length.

ON THE EDGE
A colorful anemone decorates a fissure, or crack, near where the Pacific Ocean seafloor is spreading. New floor forms faster in the Pacific than in the Atlantic because more volcanic activity occurs at the rift in the Pacific.

HOT AND SPICY
A crab ventures into the hot water of an undersea vent. Underwater volcanism heats the water to temperatures as high as 720°F.

Hot Spots

Volcanic eruptions occur far beyond the edges of plates. In some places, for reasons that scientists do not fully understand, magma burns through the the Earth's crust in the middle of a plate at a place called a hot spot, building a volcano there. This is what happened to create the Hawaiian Islands. Hot spots fuel volcanoes in the middle of continents as well.

INSTANT ISLAND

One day in 1963, an island began to rise above the waters of the North Atlantic Ocean. Magma seeped up from a rift in the ocean floor to build Surtsey, an island off Iceland. Scientists think a hot spot also contributed to the island's growth.

FURNACE PEAK

Lava spews from two vents on Piton de la Fournaise, a hot spot volcano on Réunion Island in the Indian Ocean.

The Hawaiian Islands rise from the bottom of the Pacific Ocean. Loihi, a seamount, or submarine mountain, will someday reach above the waves.

CHAIN REACTION

Volcanic mountains that form a line on the Pacific Ocean floor are created as the Pacific plate moves slowly over a hot spot. The mountains become islands of Hawaii as they reach the ocean's surface.

LEND ME SOME LAVA ▶

Lava flowing from Kilauea has added thousands of square miles to the Big Island of Hawaii and continues to build new land each year.

3 Life on the Edge

Pompeii residents left behind graffiti on their walls.

Living near a volcano can be very dangerous. That's what the people of Pompeii, a city in Italy, learned one August day in A.D. 79. Mount Vesuvius, the volcano in the town's backyard, erupted violently, spewing poisonous gas and masses of rock and ash. Vesuvius buried the entire town, taking the lives of some 2,000 Pompeiians.

REASON TO WORRY?

Like Pompeii, modern-day Naples has grown into a lively city despite having a volcano in the vicinity. Vesuvius last erupted in 1944.

DAY OF DOOM

Pompeiians flee the blasts from Mount Vesuvius. A violent earthquake 15 years earlier hinted at the destruction to come.

PICTURE PERFECT
Excavations begun in the 18th century uncovered the buildings and streets of Pompeii.

ETERNAL REST
Pumice and ash hardened around the victims of Vesuvius. Skeletons survived inside. Later filled with plaster, the casts show the final moments of Pompeii's residents.

After the plaster set, archaeologists chipped pumice and ash away, leaving plaster casts.

Volcano Power

Volcanoes certainly destroy, but they also create. Like the residents of ancient Pompeii and modern-day Naples, people choose to live near active volcanoes because volcanic ash fertilizes the soil. In addition, people from Japan to California to Iceland have harnessed geothermal energy, the heat energy generated deep within the Earth.

Hot sand beaches, the result of volcanic mineral springs, draw bathers to Beppu, a resort town on the Japanese island of Kyushu.

THANKS A BUNCH
Bananas in Iceland? Thanks to volcanic steam, tropical fruits thrive in this chilly country's greenhouses no matter what the weather is like outside.

WINE VINES
Nearby volcanoes created the perfect soil for growing wine grapes and other crops in California's fertile Napa Valley.

28

BOILING ON THE RIVER

Hot Creek lives up to its name for hikers taking a break at Long Valley Caldera in California. Volcanic hot springs provide the warmth. Long Valley is one of North America's most active volcanic areas.

POWER PLAY

Bathers enjoy Iceland's Blue Lagoon, a recreation area created by the same natural steam that fuels the energy plant in the background. Icelanders use pipes and wells to tap steam and water heated by magma.

Lands of Fire and Ice

The nation called Iceland could also be called Fireland. The ice and snow that often cover this tiny island country near the Arctic Circle hide a huge volcanic furnace that causes mountains to grow overnight and lava and gases to flow from fissures in the ground for months at a time. Yet people have lived in Iceland for more than a thousand years and have adapted to its conditions.

Lava flowing into the North Atlantic from Eldfell raised water temperatures, allowing Icelanders to take an ocean bath in January.

ESCAPE FROM ELDFELL
Residents of the Icelandic island of Heimaey flee Eldfell, the volcano built from a fissure eruption that began in January 1973. Most people left safely.

STEAMED UP
Thousands of steam vents dot the ground in Iceland's central rift area.

RIFT RIDER
Located on an exposed part of the Mid-Atlantic Ridge—a major portion of the Mid-Ocean Ridge—Iceland straddles a rift at the edge of two plates. The rift sparks eruptions in the center of the country.

LASTING LAVA
Within six months, thick lava from Eldfell destroyed a third of Vestmannaeyjar, Heimaey's only town, and added almost two square miles to the island. Workers pumped water on the lava 24 hours a day for two months and kept it from filling the harbor.

31

Active Alaska

More volcanoes burst through Alaska's icy terrain than occur in any other part of the United States. Alaska contains 44 active volcanoes, about 80 percent of the country's total. Enormous volcanic eruptions, often accompanied by earthquakes and the immense sea waves called tsunamis, have regularly rocked Alaska for thousands of years. Alaska averages two volcanic eruptions every year.

CRAZY CALDERA
Streaming lava and flows of ash and rock pour from the caldera, or large collapsed summit, of Mount Veniaminof. It ranks as one of Alaska's most active volcanoes.

WE QUIT
Created by immense eruptions in 1912, the Valley of 10,000 Smokes then held thousands of steam-producing vents that have since stopped smoking.

Ring of Fire

HOT AND COLD
Alaska sits along the Ring of Fire, the arc of volcanism rimming the Pacific Ocean. Most Alaskan volcanoes are found in the Aleutian Range, a string of mountains that stretches one thousand miles into the Bering Sea.

CHAIN SMOKER ▶
A plume of smoke billows almost continuously from Shishaldin Volcano, a graceful cone rising 9,000 feet o the Aleutian island of Unimak. The perfect composite cone of Shishaldin resembles that of Japan's Mount Fu

5 Cracked-up Krakatau

The Asian island chain of Indonesia is the most volcanically active country on Earth. Some 400 volcanoes dot an area about a fourth the size of the United States. Underneath Indonesia, one plate is diving under another. Dense rock of the diving plate melts into magma loaded with very unstable gas, creating the world's most violent eruptions. The island of Krakatau (CRACK-uh-tauw), which was located between the present-day islands of Sumatra and Java, blew to bits when the volcano erupted in 1883.

PERILOUS PADDIES
Indonesian farmers grow rice in paddies on the slopes of volcanic mountains. Despite the danger of living in the world's most active volcanic zone, Indonesia is a densely populated country. Most people are farmers, who benefit from the rich volcanic soil.

The force of Krakatau's eruption was so great that residents of Perth, Australia, some 3,000 miles away, could hear it. More than 36,000 people died as a result of the blast.

Australia

KRAKATAU'S KID
A smoking cone of ash began to grow from the remains of Krakatau beginning in 1927. Scientists expect Anakrakatau, "child of Krakatau," to someday erupt violently—as its parent did.

Global Effects

The spectacular eruptions in southeastern Asia often have long-lasting effects. Massive clouds of ash and volcanic gases rocket into the upper atmosphere, where winds blow them around the Earth. People in England viewed much redder sunsets after Krakatau erupted in 1883. Ash also dims sunlight, causing a drop in temperature and changing climate on a global scale.

CRATER COMPETITION

In 1815 Indonesia's Mount Tambora sent out so much ash that many parts of the world saw a "year without summer" in 1816. Tambora ejected four times more airborne debris than its neighbor Krakatau and 80 times more than Washington State's Mount St. Helens.

COOL CLOUDS

Ash clouds that lowered average air temperature around the world pour from Mount Pinatubo in the Philippines in June of 1991.

Vesuvius   Tambora   Krakatau   St. Helens   Pinatubo

Ruined crops brought on a food shortage in many parts of the world.

A GRAINY DAY
Pinatubo's thick ash clouds turned three days into nights in nearby villages. Then heavy rains turned the ash into mudflows that left 400,000 people homeless.

SNOWY SUMMER
Tambora's effects were felt as far away as New England, where snow fell and frost dusted crops during the summer of 1816.

6 Fiery Cascades

ost of the time, the postcard-perfect peaks of the Cascade Range in the northwestern United States hide the fact that it is part of the Ring of Fire. This young mountain range grew where a small plate of Earth's crust slides under the North American plate. Grinding down into the hot interior of the Earth, the smaller plate and overlying rock melt into magma. That magma fuels a furnace some 50 miles beneath the Cascades that at times erupts.

SNOW GO
Despite the possibility of future eruptions, skiers, snowboarders, and hikers enjoy the slopes and forests of the volcanic Cascade mountains.

IN THE HOOD
On average, once each century a Cascades peak such as Mount Hood blows its top.

CASCADES CAVERNS ▶
Steam from volcanoes sculpted a mile-long cave in the ice on Mount Rainier, a Cascades peak in Washington. The intensity of the heat varies, so the size and shape of the cave change.

39

Mount St. Helens Mayhem

It started with rumblings in the ground and a bulge that grew like an enormous blister on the mountain's north face. Scientists knew something big was going to happen, but not quite when—or what. On May 18, 1980, the wait was over. Erupting with the power of 500 atomic bombs, Mount St. Helens destroyed everything in its path for 200 square miles and took dozens of lives.

Lodge owner Harry Truman refused to abandon his hom and cats when told that Mount St. Helens would erupt. He and his pets all perished in the fiery eruption.

SO LONG, SUMMIT
The Mount St. Helens blast tore away the upper 1,300 feet of the mountain's crest. Continuing, smaller eruptions and vibrations in other area mountains remind scientists that the Cascade chain remains an active volcanic range.

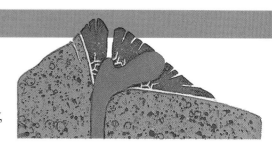

BLISTER
A large bulge on the north side of Mount St. Helens grew day by day, signaling a big change.

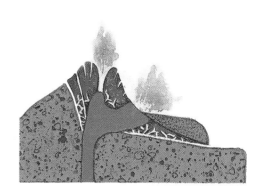

LANDSLIDE
A May 18 earthquake collapsed the bulge, triggering a huge landslide toward the North Toutle River.

BLAST
Within seconds, repeated blasts of glassy ash, rock, gas, steam, and sticky lava erupted upward and sideways.

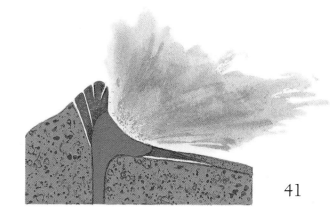

SURGE
Clouds of steam and 400 million tons of pulverized rock dust filled the atmosphere. A mix of superheated gas and ash roared down the slopes, burying everything in its path.

41

Day of Destruction

Racing away from the scene in his car, a photographer snapped this menacing cloud of superheated ash, rock, and gas as it tore down the slopes of Mount St. Helens at 200 miles an hour. Called pyroclastic flow, the deadly combination of volcanic products poses more of a threat to life and property than typical lava flow. Poisonous gas and hot, thick ash travel at speeds so great they kill everything in their path.

43

Return to Life

The eruption of Mount St. Helens turned a flourishing forest into a gray wasteland. The blast mowed down 200 square miles of trees, snapping the trunks like matchsticks. Some two million animals died. Yet within weeks, small signs of life began to return. Now, more than 20 years later, plants and animals are beginning to thrive again. It will be centuries, however, before the fully forested wilderness returns.

NOT YET
Some areas near Mount St. Helens remain off limits to hikers and other visitors. The land needs more time to recover.

FROM FIRE TO FIRE
Bright pink blossoms of fireweed announce the return of life to Mount St. Helens. This hardy plant is often the first vegetation to return to areas destroyed by volcanic eruptions or forest fires.

UNLUCKY LAKE
Totalled trees and mud choked Spirit Lake after the blast. New life pokes through on shores where tall evergreens stood.

THAT'S THE SPIRIT ▶
Spirit Lake shows the promise of a comeback. Scientists have learned much about nature's recovery plan from the Mount St. Helens blast. They have been amazed at the rapid return of some animal populations, such as elk.

 # Volcanic Variations

Volcanic activity creates a variety of landforms, some quite different from the familiar smoking cones of volcanic mountains. All the formations start with molten rock inside the Earth. Sometimes the rock oozes out like toothpaste through cracks in the ground. Or it can spread over the land like a spilled bowl of cake batter.

The columns extend 600 feet into the Irish Sea.

SHIP ROCK

Lava that plugged the neck of an ancient volcano in New Mexico rises like a sailing ship after the outer slopes have eroded.

GIANTS CAUSEWAY

Volcanoes in northeastern Ireland produced thousands of rock columns that legend says formed a bridge for giants to cross dry-footed to Scotland.

CRATER LAKE

When Mount Mazama, in the Cascades of Oregon, blew its top some 7,000 years ago, it left a huge caldera. The 1,900-foot-deep hole eventually filled with crystal-clear water. Another cone rises as an island in the lake.

DOWN THE TUBE!!

Lava tubes often form when hot, runny lava forms a crust that cools and hardens quickly. The lava inside drains out, leaving a tunnel.

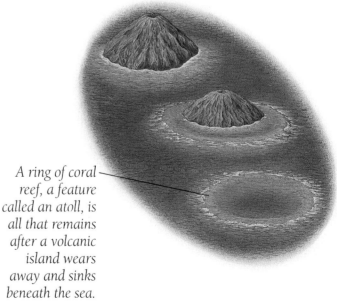

A ring of coral reef, a feature called an atoll, is all that remains after a volcanic island wears away and sinks beneath the sea.

SUPER SIZED

A reminder of million-year-old volcanic activity, 60-foot-high columns called the Devils Postpile rise at the base of California's Sierra Nevada mountains.

47

STEP DOWN

The boiling waters of Mammoth Hot Springs dissolve underground rock. When the waters rise to the surface, they deposit minerals from the dissolved rock in step-like terraces. Bacteria and algae in the water color the formation.

STEAM TABLE

In winter, elk and other creatures find food and warmth near Yellowstone's geothermal features. The heat melts snow and ice, exposing vegetation the animals need to survive the freezing weather.

8 Africa Apart

AFRICAN GIANT
The icy summit of volcanic Mount Kilimanjaro soars 19,340 feet just beyond the African Rift. Kilimanjaro is the continent's highest mountain.

Volcanism is tearing Africa apart. Just as a rift system is pushing the ocean floor apart at the Mid-Ocean Ridge, a rift system in eastern Africa is causing the Earth's second largest continent to split. One part of the African plate is breaking away very slowly. A central portion of the rift has collapsed. The weakened crust in the area allows magma to surface, giving birth to volcanoes inside and outside the rift.

CREATURE FEATURE
Wildlife thrives in Tanzania's Ngorongoro (IN-gore-un-gore-o) Crater, a 12-mile-wide collapsed volcano. Some people call the huge caldera "zoo-in- a-volcano"!

Scientists are not sure why a volcano in Kenya produces ash that, when rained on, turns into washing soda, an ingredient used in detergent.

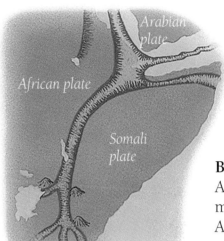

BREAKING UP

Africa began to split some 25 million years ago, when the Arabian plate started to pull away from the African one. The Red Sea flows in from the north. Eventually it will divide the two sections of Africa.

PRETTY IN PINK

Flamingoes gather at a lake in Ngorongoro Crater. The crater's wall, up to 2,000 feet high, rises in the background.

Blasts in Space

Earth isn't the only planet with a volcanic past, present, or future. Several planets in the solar system, and their moons, show signs of the volcanic activity found on Earth. Earth's moon, for example, has mountains, craters, and lava flows almost four billion years old. On some planets, volcanoes have long been silent. On Io, one of the planet Jupiter's moons, cameras on space probes have captured volcanic activity.

MEGA MOUNTAINS
Earth's tallest peaks—Asia's Himalaya and Mauna Kea, a Hawaiian volcano that rises 33,476 feet from the seafloor—seem puny compared to 65,000-foot Olympus Mons on Mars.

MOON GLOW
Active volcanoes erupt on Io, one of Jupiter's 16 moons. Gases and other material burst 160 miles above Io's surface. About the size of Earth's moon, Io gets its orange-yellow color from the sulfur produced by these eruptions.

WHERE IT'S AT
Mercury, Venus, Earth, Mars, Earth's moon, and Jupiter's moon Io share a volcanic past. Besides Earth, only Io shows active volcanoes.

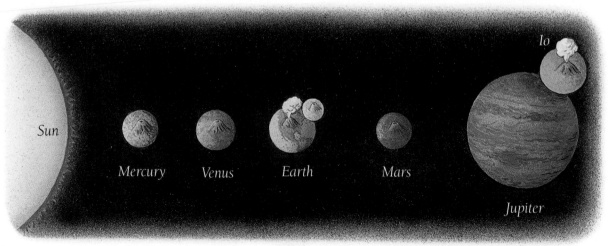

Sun Mercury Venus Earth Mars Jupiter Io

BIG BLAST ▶
Maat Mons soars 5.2 miles above the surface of Venus, making it the second highest peak on that planet. Volcanic craters and those caused by meteorite impacts pock the Venusian surface.

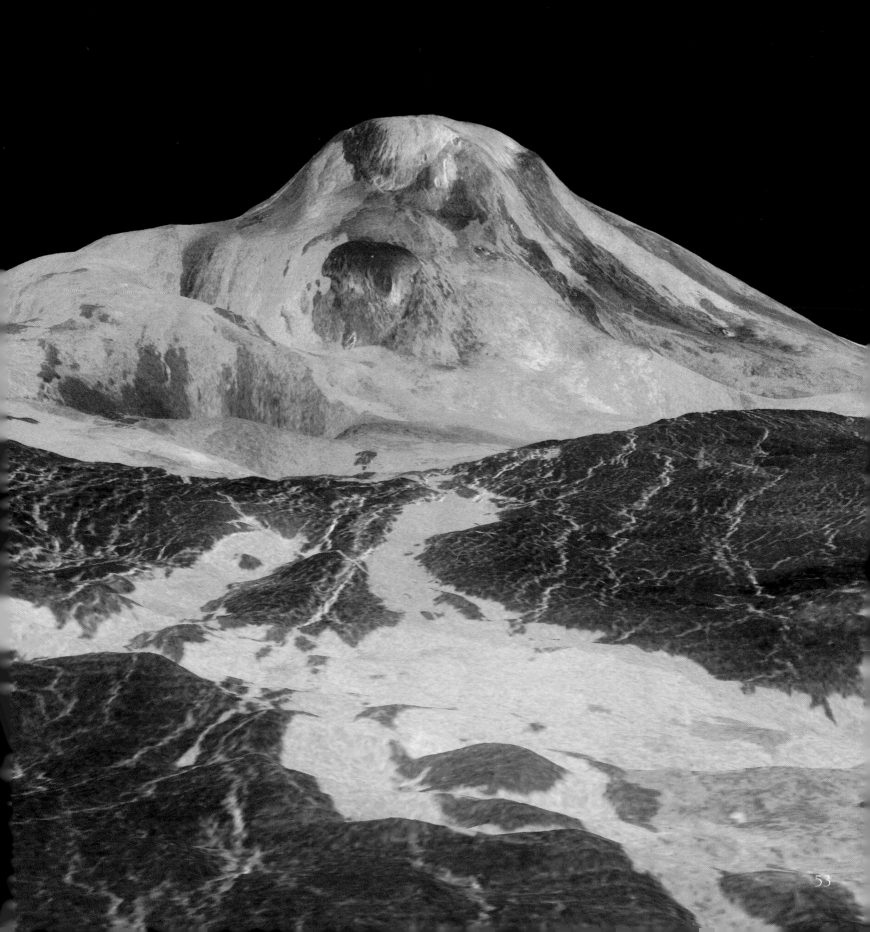

10 Taming the Dragon

Scientists try to learn everything they can about volcanoes. That knowledge helps them predict when volcanoes might erupt so that they can give advance warning to people who live in harm's way. Since studying volcanoes can be dangerous work, technology is often used for close encounters. Some active volcanoes, such as Mauna Loa on Hawaii, are home to permanent research stations.

LEAVING HOME
Successful prediction allowed residents of a village on the island of Hawaii to evacuate with many of their possessions before a Kilauea eruption.

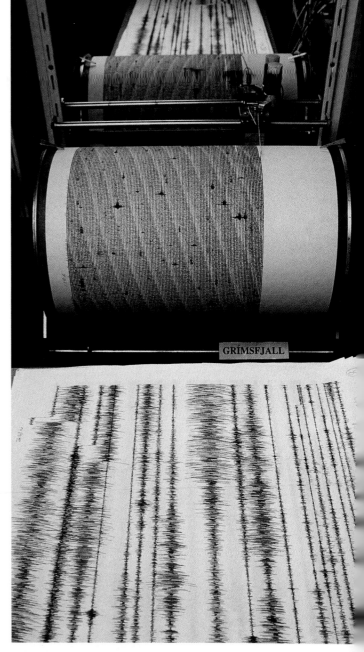

GRÍMSFJALL

SIZING IT UP
A seismograph (SIZE-muh-graf) records vibrations that might announce an eruption. A revolving drum is anchored in bedrock, solid rock under the soil. If the rock moves, so does the drum, but a pen on it stays in place, recording the vibrations in wavy lines.

EARTH WALK
Designed to explore other planets, this NASA robot works on Earth as well. It can navigate on hot and sticky terrain, collecting volcanic gas and rocks in spots way too warm for humans to handle.

A SUITABLE JOB
Protected by a shiny suit, a scientist can get near enough to a lava flow to poke in a probe and obtain information such as its temperature and gas content.

Did You Know...

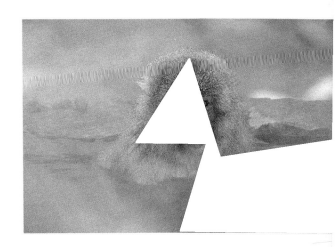

1 **THAT** snow monkeys in Japan often hang out in hot springs—nature's hot tubs. The springs allow these monkeys to live farther north than usual, surviving cold and snowy winters. Thermal springs formed by volcanic activity are found throughout the islands of Japan.

2 **THAT** the ancient Romans believed volcanoes were the work of their blacksmith-god, Vulcan. When an island in the Mediterranean began to erupt some 2,000 years ago, the Romans attributed the smoke and fire to Vulcan's underground workshop. The Romans named the island Vulcano, and a form of that word came to be used to describe all fiery eruptions.

3 **THAT** in 1943 a farmer in southern Mexico watched one day as a volcano suddenly began to grow in his cornfield. Within a year, the Paricutín volcano stood more than 1,000 feet high. Paricutín stopped erupting in 1952.

4 **THAT** lava pouring into the ocean can form rafts. As lava that contains a lot of gas bubbles cools, it become a porous rock called pumice. Pumice rafts float, can hold passengers, and can travel great distances. Some have been found 4,000 miles from their source.

5 **THAT** volcanic eruptions can turn trees to stone? During an eruption, hot lava flows cover the trees, killing them. Then the lava hardens and turns into tree-shaped rock. When living things return to the landscape, these ghostly forms remain.

6 **THAT** a prisoner in the local jail was one of only two survivors during a 1902 eruption of Mount Pelée. It devastated the port of St. Pierre in Martinique and killed 30,000 people. The man survived because his cell had thick walls and faced the direction opposite to the blast.

Glossary

ATMOSPHERE The layer of gases surrounding a planet.

CALDERA A large depression on a volcano, often caused when the summit of a volcanic mountain collapses. Calderas are larger than craters and are usually more than a mile wide.

CONTINENT One of the main divisions of land on Earth. The seven continents are Asia, Africa, North America, South America, Antarctica, Europe, and Australia.

CONE A mountain, often with steep sides, built by repeated volcanic eruptions in one place and made of layers of lava, cinders, and/or ash.

CORE The hot, innermost layer of the Earth.

CRATER The enlarged and usually bowl-shaped opening at or near the top of a volcano from which lava, ashes, and gases are ejected. Also, a depression made by the impact of a meteorite.

CRUST The rocky, outermost layer of the Earth.

EJECTA Any kind of material that is ejected from a volcano during an eruption, including lava, ash, and various types of rocks.

FISSURE A narrow crack in the Earth that emits lava and other volcanic material.

FUMAROLE A vent or opening in the surface of the Earth that emits steam.

GEOTHERMAL Produced by the heat of Earth's interior.

GEYSER A hot spring through which jets of water and steam erupt.

HOT SPOT An intensely hot region in the middle of a plate where magma may burn through the Earth's crust and form a volcano.

HOT SPRING A place where water heated by a magma chamber rises to the surface and collects or flows out of the ground.

MAGMA Hot, melted rock within the Earth.

MANTLE The middle layer of the Earth, made of hot rock.

MID-OCEAN RIDGE An underwater mountain range that extends through Earth's oceans and is formed where plates of the Earth's crust are pulling apart.

MINERAL A nonliving element or compound, such as iron, calcium, or sodium chloride, that is found in nature.

MUD POT A place where water heated by an underground magma chamber trickles to the surface, forming a small pool of bubbling mud.

PLATE One of many huge, rocky slabs that make up the outer shell of the Earth.

RIFT A large crack on the surface of the Earth or on the seafloor caused by plates pulling away from each other.

SILICA A mineral composed of silicon and oxygen that is a major component of sand and of volcanic rocks.

VENT An opening in the Earth through which lava, ashes, and gases erupt. Also, an opening that channels volcanically heated water and/or steam.

Index

Boldface indicates illustrations.

Credits

scoria

Published by
The National Geographic Society
John M. Fahey, Jr., *President
and Chief Executive Officer*
Gilbert M. Grosvenor,
  Chairman of the Board
Nina D. Hoffman,
  President, Books and School Publishing

Staff for this Book
Barbara Brownell, *Director of Continuities*
Marianne R. Koszorus, *Director of Layout and Design*
Toni Eugene, *Editor*
Alexandra Littlehales, *Art Director*
Susan V. Kelly, *Illustrations Editor*
Catherine Herbert Howell, *Researcher*
Carl Mehler, *Director of Maps*
Melissa Hunsiker, *Assistant Editor*
Sharon Kocsis Berry, *Illustrations Assistant*
Anne K. McCain, *Indexer*
Mark A. Caraluzzi, *Vice President, Sales and Marketing*
Heidi Vincent, *Director, Direct Marketing*
Vincent P. Ryan, *Manufacturing Manager*
Lewis R. Bassford, *Production Project Manager*

Acknowledgments

We are grateful for the assistance of Peter B. Stifel, associate
professor emeritus, University of Maryland, College Park,
Scientific Consultant.

COVER: The Italian volcano Stromboli, which anchors an
island in the Mediterranean Sea, last erupted in 1998.

Illustrations Credits

COVER: Ingo Arndt/Tom ?????
Front Matter: 1 E. R. Degginger/Earth Scenes; 2-3 Victoria McCormick; 4 (top-bottom) Mark Thiessen, NGS Staff Photographer; Dr. Robert R. Hessler; Roger Ressmeyer; Harold E. Wilson/Earth Scenes; 5 (top) Photo Researchers/Philipe Bourseiller; (top center left) John Gerlach/Earth Scenes; (top center right) James H. Robinson/Earth Scenes; (bottom center left) JPL; (bottom center right) Phyllis Greenberg/Animals Animals; (botom) USGS; 8 John Fletcher; 9 James Watt/Earth Scenes; 10 (top) Robert Cremins; (left) Carol Schwartz; (r) James Brandt/Earth Scenes; 11 (left) E.R. Degginger/Earth Scenes; (right) Victoria McCormick/Earth Scenes; 12 (all) Carol Schwartz; 13 (top) Robert Cremins; (bottom) Phil Degginger
Volcanoes Rock: 14 (top) Mark Thiessen, NGS Staff Photographer; (left) Carol Schwartz; (right) Michael Andrews/Earth Scenes; 15 ©R. Toms/OSF/Earth Scenes; 16 (top) Robert Cremins; (bottom) Leonard L.T. Rhodes; 17 (left) David C. Fritts/Earth Scenes; (right) Paul Chesley; (bottom) Carol Schwartz; 18 (top) Donna Ikenbury; (bottom) Carol Schwartz; 19 (top) Robert Cremins; (bottom) C.C Lockwood/Earth Scenes
Under the Sea: 20-1 Robert Cremins; 22 (left) Robert Cremins; (right) Dr. Robert R. Hessler; 23 (top) Woods Hole; (bottom) Dr. Robert R. Hessler; 24 (left) Carol Schwartz; (top) Solarfilma; (bottom) R.B. Trombley, Southwest Volcano Research Centre; 25 E.R. Degginer/Earth Scenes
Life on the Edge: 26 (left & top) Robert Cremins; (bottom) David Alan Harvey; 27 (top) James L. Stanfield; (bottom) Lisa Vazquez; 28 (left) Robert Cremins; (right) Bob Krist; (bottom) Michael Dick/Animals Animals; (top) ©Brooks Walker; (bottom) Roger Ressmeyer
Lands of Fire and Ice: 30 (left) Solarfilma; (top) Robert Cremins; (bottom) Francis Lepine/Earth Scenes; 31 (top) E.R. Degginger/Earth Scenes; (bottom) Carol Schwartz; 32 (left) Carol Schwartz; (top) Harold E. Wilson/Earth Scenes; (bottom) David C. Fritts/Earth Scenes; 33 Harold E. Wilson/Earth Scenes
Cracked-up Krakatau: 34 Robert Cremins; 34-5 Dani/Jeske/Earth Scenes; 35 Robert Cremins; 36 (top) Shawn G. Henry; (bottom) Carol Schwartz; 37 (top) Robert Cremins; (bottom) Photo Researchers/Philippe Bourseiller
Fiery Cascades: (left) Robert Cremins; (tight) Michael Andrews/Earth Scenes; 39 Eugene Kiver; 40 (top) Robert Cremins; (bottom) C.C. Lockwood/Earth Scenes; 41 (left, all) Earth Images; (right, all) Robert Cremins; 42 Gary Rosenquist/Earth Images; 44 (left) David Boyle/Earth Scenes; (top) Robert Cremins; (bottom) James H. Robinson/Earth Scenes; 45 Patti Murray/Earth Scenes
Volcanic Variations: 46 (left) Michael Andrews/Earth Scenes; (right) Robert Cremins; (bottom) Breck P. Kent/Earth Scenes; 47 (left) John Gerlach/Earth Scenes; (top) Roger Aitkenhead/Earth Scenes; (bottom) Carol Schwartz; 48 (left) Robert Cremins; (right) Norbert Rosing/Earth Scenes; 49 (top) Ken Cole/Animals Animals; (bottom) M. Fogden/OSF/Earth Scenes
Africa Apart: 50 (top) Ken Cole/Earth Scenes; (bottom) Robert Cremins; 51 (left) Robert Cremins; (right) Carol Schwartz; (bottom) Phyllis Greenberg/Animals Animals
Blasts in Space: 52 (top) Carol Schwartz; (center) NGS Image Collection; (bottom) Carol Schwartz; 53 Jet Propulsion Laboratory
Taming the Dragon: (left) Robert Cremins; (right) Steve Winter; 54 (top) Carol Schwartz; (bottom) USGS
Back Matter: 56 (top) Ralph Reinhold; (center) Robert Cremins; (bottom) Library of Congress; 57 (top) Robert Cremins; (center) Bruce Davidson/Earth Scenes; (bottom) Robert Cremins; 60 Breck P. Kent/Earth Scenes

Composition for this book by the National Geographic Society Book Division. Printed and bound by R.R. Donnelley & Sons Company, Willard, Ohio. Color separations by Quad Graphics, Martinsburg, West Virginia. Case cover printed by Miken Companies, Cheektowaga, New York.

Library of Congress CIP Data
Howell, Catherine Herbert
  Volcano / by Catherine Herbert Howell
    p.   cm — (National Geographic nature library)
  Includes bibliographical references and index.
  Summary: Presents information on the formation, various types, and specific examples
of volcanoes.
  ISBN 0-7922-7580-2
  1. Volcanoes—Juvenile literature. [1. Volcanoes] I. Title. II. Series.

QE521.3.H69   2001
551.21—dc21

200103269